The Last Straw

by Paula Palangi

Illustrated by Linda Graves

Chariot Books
David C. Cook Publishing Co.

Chariot Books™ is an imprint of David C. Cook Publishing Co.
David C. Cook Publishing Co., Elgin, Illinois 60120
David C. Cook Publishing Co., Weston, Ontario
Nova Distribution Ltd., Torquay, England

THE LAST STRAW
© 1992 by Paula Palangi for text and Linda Graves for illustrations

Designed by Terry Julien
First Printing, 1992
Printed in the United States of America
96 95 94 93 92   5 4 3 2 1

Library of Congress Cataloging-in-Publication Data
Palangi, Paula.
The last straw / Paula Palangi.
              p.   cm.
Summary: Winter squabbling in the McDonald household turns to a true celebration of
the Christmas spirit when Mother revives an old holiday custom of doing favors in secret
for other family members.
ISBN 0-7814-0562-9
1. Christmas stories, American. [1. Christmas—Fiction. 2. Family life—Fiction.]
I. Title.
PS3566.A456L37   1992
813'.54—dc20
[Fic]   91-44346
                                CIP
                                AC

This book belongs to

_____

It was another long, winter afternoon with everyone stuck in the house. And the four little McDonalds were at it again—bickering, teasing, fighting over their toys.

At times like these, Mother was almost ready to believe that her children didn't love each other, even though she knew that wasn't really true. All brothers and sisters fight, of course, but lately her lively little bunch had been particularly horrible to each other, especially Eric and Kelly who were just a year apart. They seemed determined to spend the whole long winter making each other miserable. Pick, pick, pick. Squabble, squabble, squabble.

"Gimme that. It's mine!"

"Is not, fatso! I had it first!"

Mother sighed as she listened to the latest argument coming from the living room. With Christmas only a month away, the McDonald house seemed sadly lacking in Christmas spirit. This was supposed to be the season of sharing and love, of warm feelings and

happy hearts. But where were those warm feelings and happy hearts? A home needed more than just pretty packages or twinkling lights on the tree to fill

it with the Christmas spirit. But how could any mother convince her children that being kind to each other was the most important way to get ready for Christmas?

Mother had only one idea. Years ago her grandmother had told her about an old Christmas custom that helped people discover the real meaning of Christmas. Perhaps it would

work for her family this year. It was certainly worth a try.

Mother gathered her four little rascals together and sat them down on the stairs, smallest to tallest—Mike, Randi, Kelly, and Eric. "How would you kids like to start a new Christmas project this year?" she asked. "It's like a game, but it can only be played by people who can keep a secret. Can everyone here do that?"

"I can!" shouted Eric, wildly waving his arm in the air.

"I can keep a secret better than he can," yelled Kelly, jumping up and waving her arms in the air, too. If there were going to be any kind of a contest, Kelly wanted to make sure she beat Eric.

"I can do it!" chimed in Randi, not quite sure what was happening but not wanting to be left out either.

"Me, too, me, too, me, too," squealed little Mike, bouncing up and down. "I'm big enough."

"Well then, here's how the game works," Mother explained. "This year we're going to surprise baby

Jesus when He comes on Christmas Eve by making Him the softest bed in the world. We're going to build a little crib for Him to sleep in right here in our house and fill it with straw to make it comfortable. But here's the secret part. The straw we put in the manger will measure all the kind things we do between now and Christmas. We just can't tell anyone who we're doing the good things for."

The children looked confused. "But how will baby Jesus know it's His bed?"

"He'll know," said Mother. "He'll recognize it by the love we put in it to make it soft. And He'll be happy to sleep there."

"But who will we do the kind things for?" asked Eric, who was still a little confused.

"It's simple," said Mother. "We'll do them for each other. Once every week between now and Christmas, we'll put all of our names in this hat, mine and Daddy's, too. Then we'll do kind things for the person whose name we get for a whole week. But here's

the hard part. We can't tell anyone else whose name we draw for that week. We'll each try to do as many favors for our special person as we can without getting caught. And for every secret good thing we do, we'll put another straw in the crib."

"Like being a spy!" squealed Randi. "I can do that! I'm a good spy."

"But what if I pick someone who I don't like?" frowned Kelly.

Mother thought about that for a minute. "Maybe you could use extra fat straws for those good things because they just might be harder to do. But think how much faster the fat straws will fill up our crib. Then on Christmas Eve we'll put baby Jesus in His little bed, and He'll sleep that night on a mattress made of love. I think He'd like that, don't you?

"Now, who will build a little crib for us?" she asked.

Eric was the oldest and the only one allowed to use the tools alone, so he marched off to the basement to try. There were banging noises and sawing noises,

and for a long time there were no noises at all. But finally, Eric climbed back up the stairs with a proud smile. "The best crib in the world!" he grinned. "And I did it all myself."

For once, everyone agreed. The little manger *was* the best crib in the world, even though one leg was an inch too short and the crib rocked a bit. But it had been built with love—and about a hundred bent nails—so it would certainly last a long time.

"Now we need straw," said Mother, and together they tumbled out to the car to go looking for some.

Surprisingly, no one fought over who was going to sit in the front seat that day as they drove around searching for an empty field. At last they spotted a small, empty lot that had been covered with tall grass in the summer. Now that it was December, the dried, yellow stalks looked just like real straw.

Mother stopped the car, and, even though it was a bitter-cold day, the kids scrambled out to pick handfuls of the tall grass.

"That's enough!" Mother finally laughed when the cardboard box in the trunk was almost overflowing. "Remember, it's only a small crib." So home they went to spread their straw carefully on a tray Mother had put on the kitchen table. The empty manger was placed gently on top, and no one could even notice that it had one short leg.

"When can we pick names? When can we pick?" shouted the children, their faces still rosy from the cold.

"As soon as Daddy comes home for dinner," Mother answered.

At the supper table that night, the six names were written on separate pieces of paper, folded up, shuffled and shaken around in an old baseball hat, and the drawing began.

Kelly picked first and immediately started to giggle. Randi reached into the hat next, trying hard to look like a serious spy. Daddy glanced at his scrap of paper and smiled quietly behind his hand. Mother picked out a name, but her face never gave away a clue. Next, little Mike reached into the hat, but since he couldn't read yet Daddy had to whisper in his ear and tell him which name he had picked. Mike then quickly ate his little scrap of paper so no one would ever find out who his secret person was. Eric was the last to choose, and as he unfolded his piece of paper a frown crossed his face. But he stuffed the name quickly into his pocket and said nothing. The family was ready to begin.

The week that followed was filled with surprises. It

seemed the McDonald house had suddenly been invaded by an army of invisible elves, and good things were happening everywhere. Kelly would walk into her room at bedtime and find her little blue nightgown neatly laid out and her bed turned down. Someone cleaned up the sawdust under the workbench without being asked. The jelly blobs disappeared magically from the kitchen counter after lunch one day while Mother was out getting the mail. And every morning, while Eric was brushing his teeth, someone crept quietly into his room and made his bed. It wasn't made perfectly, but it was made. That particular little elf must have had very short arms because he couldn't seem to reach all the way to the middle.

"Where are my shoes?" asked Daddy one morning. No one seemed to know, but before he left for work, they were back in the closet, all shined up.

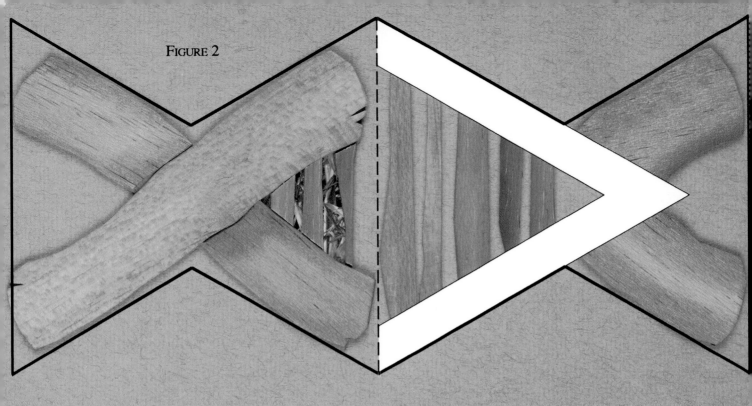

FIGURE 2

1. Remove both pages with the manger from the book.

2. Cut out figures 1, 2, and 3 along the heavy lines.

3. Fold figures 1 and 2 in half along the dotted line. With printed side out, glue the two halves together. (See diagram.)

4. Fold figure 3 along the dotted lines so that the tabs fold in and the printed side faces out.

5. Glue tabs from figure 3 to figures 1 and 2, making sure the sides are even so the manger will stand. (See diagram.)

6. Your manger is now ready to be filled with straw and love.

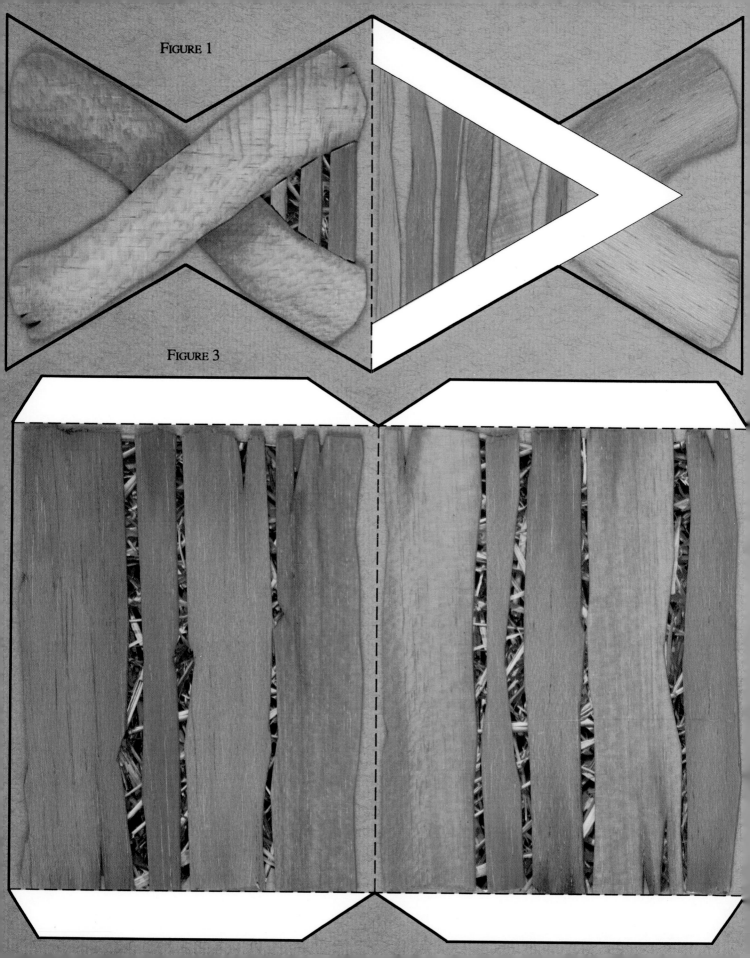

Figure 1

Figure 3

Mother noticed other changes during that week, too. The children weren't teasing or fighting as much. An argument would start and then suddenly stop right in the middle for no apparent reason. Even Eric and Kelly seemed to be getting along better and bickering less. In fact, all the children could be seen smiling secret smiles and giggling to themselves at times. And slowly, one by one, pieces of straw began to appear in the little crib. At first there were just a few, but then a few more appeared each day. By the end of the first week, there was actually a little pile in the crib. Now, mind you, no one ever saw the straws go in, but later the children could be seen patting and testing the tiny pile for softness.

By Sunday everyone was anxious to pick new names again, and this time there was more laughter and merriment during the picking process than there had been the first time, except for Eric. Once again he unfolded his piece of paper, looked at it, and stuffed it in his pocket without a word. Mother noticed, as mothers always do, but said nothing.

The second week brought more amazing events! The garbage was taken out without anyone being asked. Someone even did two of Kelly's hard math problems one night when she left her homework out on the table.

The little pile of straw grew higher and softer. Everyone seemed to be watching and checking it carefully each day. With only two weeks left until Christmas, the children wondered if their homemade bed would be comfortable enough for baby Jesus when He came.

"Who will be baby Jesus anyway?" Randi asked on the third Sunday night after they had all picked new names. "What can we use?"

"Perhaps we can use one of the dolls," said Mother.

"Why don't you and Mike be in charge of picking out the right one?"

The two youngest children ran off to gather up their favorite dolls, but everyone else wanted to help pick baby Jesus, too. Little Mike dragged his Bozo the Clown rag doll from his room and proudly handed it over, sniffling later when everybody laughed. Soon Eric's well-hugged teddy bear, Bruffles, joined the dolls filling up the couch. Barbie and Ken were there, along with Kermit the Frog, a pile of soft, stuffed dogs and lambs, and even a cuddly monkey that Grandma and Grandpa had sent Mike one year. But none of them seemed quite right.

Only an old baby doll, who had been loved almost to pieces, looked like a possibility for their baby Jesus. Chatty Baby she had once been called, before she stopped chatting forever after too many baths.

"But she looks funny now," said Randi. And it was true; she did look funny. Once, while playing beauty shop, Kelly had cut her own blonde hair along with Chatty Baby's, giving them both a raggedy crew cut. Kelly's hair had eventually grown back, but Chatty Baby's never had, and now the wisps of blonde hair that stuck out all over her head made her look a little lost and forgotten. But her eyes were still bright blue and she still smiled, even though her face was slightly smudged from the touch of so many chubby little fingers.

"I think she's perfect," said Mother. "Baby Jesus probably didn't have much hair when He was born either. And I'll bet He'd like to be represented by a doll who's had so many hugs."

So it was decided, and the children began to make a new outfit for their baby Jesus—a little leather vest out of scraps and some cloth diapers, because none of them quite knew what swaddling clothes were supposed to look like. But baby Jesus looked just fine in His new clothes, and best of all, He fit perfectly into the little crib. Since it wasn't quite time for Him to sleep there yet, He was laid carefully on a shelf in the hall closet to wait for Christmas Eve and a softer bed.

Meanwhile, the pile of straws grew and grew. Every day brought new and different surprises as the secret elves stepped up their activity. There was more laughter, less teasing, and hardly any mean-ness around the house. The McDonald home was finally filled with the Christmas spirit. Only Eric had been unusually quiet since the third week of name picking, and sometimes Mother would catch him looking a little sad and unhappy. But the straws in the manger continued to pile up.

At last it was almost Christmas. The final Sunday night of name picking was the night before Christmas Eve. As the family sat around the table waiting for the last set of names to be shaken in the hat, Mother said, "You've all done a wonderful job. There must be hundreds of straws in our crib—maybe a thousand. You should be so pleased with the bed you've made. But remember, there's still one whole day left. We all have time to do a little more to make the bed even softer before tomorrow night. Let's try."

The children smiled as they looked at their fluffy pile of straw. No one needed to test it anymore. They all knew it was comfortable and soft. But maybe they could still make it a little deeper, a little softer. They were going to try.

For the last time the hat was passed around the table. Little Mike picked out a name, Daddy whispered it to him, then Mike quickly ate the paper just as he had done every week. Randi unfolded hers

carefully under the table, peeked at it, and then hunched up her little shoulders, smiling. Kelly reached into the hat and giggled happily when she saw the name. Mother and Dad each took their turns, too, and then handed the hat with the last name to Eric. But as he unfolded the small scrap of paper and read it, his face pinched up and he suddenly seemed about to cry. Without a word, he turned and ran from the room.

Everyone immediately jumped up from the table, but Mother stopped them. "No! Stay where you are," she said. "Let me talk to him alone first."

Just as she reached the top of the stairs, Eric's door banged open. He was trying to pull his coat on with one hand while he carried a small, cardboard suitcase with the other hand.

"I have to leave," he said quietly through his tears. "If I don't, I'll spoil Christmas for everyone."

"But why? And where are you going?" asked Mother.

"I can sleep in my snow fort for a couple of days. I'll come home right after Christmas. I promise."

Mother started to say something about freezing and snow and no mittens or boots, but Daddy, who was now standing just behind her, put his hand on her arm and shook his head. The front door closed, and together they watched from the window as the little figure with the sadly slumped shoulders and no hat trudged across the street and sat down on a snowbank near the corner. It was very dark outside, and cold, and a few snow flurries drifted down on the small boy and his suitcase.

"But he'll freeze!" said Mother.

"Give him a few minutes alone," said Dad quietly. "I think he needs that. Then you can talk to him."

The huddled figure was already dusted with white when Mother walked across the street ten minutes later and sat down beside him on the snowbank.

"What is it, Eric? You've been so good these last weeks, but I know something's been bothering you since we first started the crib. Can you tell me, honey?"

"Ah, Mom . . . don't you see?" he sniffled. "I tried so hard, but I can't do it anymore, and now I'm going to wreck Christmas for everyone." With that he burst into sobs and threw himself into his mother's arms.

"But I don't understand," Mother said, brushing the snow and tears from his face. "What can't you do? And how could you possibly spoil Christmas for us?"

"Mom," the little boy choked, "you just don't know. I got Kelly's name *all four weeks!* And I hate Kelly! I can't do one more nice thing for her or I'll

die! I tried, Mom. I really did. I snuck in her room every night and fixed her bed. I even laid out her crummy nightgown. I emptied her wastebasket, and I didn't take a single piece of gum when it was lying right there on her desk. I did some homework for her one night when she was going to the bathroom. Mom, I even let her use my race car one day, but she smashed it right into the wall like always!

"I tried to be nice to her, Mom. Even when she called me a stupid dummy because the crib leg was short, I didn't hit her. And every week, when we picked new names, I thought it would be over. But tonight, when I got her name again, I knew I couldn't do it anymore. I can't do one more nice thing for her, Mom. I just can't! If I try, I'll probably punch her instead. And tomorrow's Christmas Eve. If I stay home and beat up Kelly, I'll spoil Christmas for everybody just when we're ready to put baby Jesus in the crib. Don't you see why I had to leave? Maybe it's not so hard for other people to be nice."

They sat together quietly for a few minutes, Mother's arm around the small boy's shoulders. Only an occasional sniffle and hiccup broke the silence on the snowbank.

Finally, Mother spoke softly. "Eric, I'm so proud of you. Every good thing you did should count double because it was especially hard for you to be nice to Kelly for so long. But you did those good things anyway, one straw at a time. You gave your love when it wasn't easy to give. Maybe that's what the spirit of Christmas is really all about. If it's too easy to give, maybe we're not really giving much of ourselves after all. And maybe it's the *hard* good things and the difficult straws that make that little crib really special.

"You're the one who's probably added the most important straws, and you can be proud of yourself. Now, how would you like a chance to earn a few easy straws like the rest of us? I still have the name I picked tonight in my pocket, and I haven't looked at

it yet. Why don't we switch, just for the last day? It will be our secret."

"That's not cheating?"

"It's not cheating," Mother smiled.

Together they dried the tears, brushed off the snow, and walked back to the house.

The next day the whole family was busy cooking and straightening up the house for Christmas Day, wrapping last-minute presents, and trying hard to keep from bursting with excitement. But even with all the activity and eagerness, a flurry of new straws piled up in the crib, and by nightfall it was almost overflowing. At different times while passing by, each member of the family, big and small, would pause and look at the wonderful pile for a moment, then smile

before going on. At last, it was almost time for the tiny crib to be used. But . . . who could really know? One more straw might still make a difference.

For that very reason, just before bedtime, Mother tiptoed quietly to Kelly's room to lay out the little blue nightgown and turn down the bed. But she stopped in the doorway, surprised. Someone had already been there. The nightgown was laid neatly across the bed, and a small red race car rested next to it on the pillow.

The last straw was Eric's after all.